THE AMAZING ADVENTURES OF THE

DC SUPER-PETS!™

Whatzit vs. the Ice Blaster Burglar

by Steve Korté
illustrated by Art Baltazar

PICTURE WINDOW BOOKS
a capstone imprint

Published by Picture Window Books, an imprint of Capstone.
1710 Roe Crest Drive
North Mankato, Minnesota 56003
capstonepub.com

Library of Congress Cataloging-in-Publication Data
Names: Korté, Steven, author. | Baltazar, Art, illustrator.
Title: Whatzit vs. the ice blaster burglar / by Steve Korte ;
illustrated by Art Baltazar.
Other titles: Whatzit versus the ice blaster burglar
Description: North Mankato, Minnesota : Picture Window Books, an imprint
of Capstone, [2021] | Series: The amazing adventures of the DC super-pets
| Audience: Ages 5–7. | Audience: Grades K–1. | Summary: "The Ice-Blue
Diamond has been stolen! Bad guy Captain Cold and his ice blaster have
given Central City the slip. When The Flash calls for backup, his superpowered
turtle, Whatzit, dashes in to save the day"—Provided by publisher.
Identifiers: LCCN 2021002844 (print) | LCCN 2021002845 (ebook) |
ISBN 9781515882589 (hardcover) | ISBN 9781515883678 (paperback) |
ISBN 9781515892328 (pdf) | ISBN 9781515893165 (kindle edition)
Subjects: CYAC: Superheroes—Fiction. | Turtles—Fiction. | Pets—Fiction.
Classification: LCC PZ7.K8385 Wh 2021 (print) | LCC PZ7.K8385 (ebook) |
DDC [E]—dc23
LC record available at https://lccn.loc.gov/2021002844
LC ebook record available at https://lccn.loc.gov/2021002845

Designed by Ted Williams
Design Elements by Shutterstock/SilverCircle

TABLE OF CONTENTS

He is known by many names,
including The Scarlet Shell and
The Fastest Turtle Alive.
He is a loyal friend to The Flash.
These are . . .

THE AMAZING
ADVENTURES OF
The Terrific
Whatzit!

CHAPTER 1

Cold Crime

It is a sunny morning in downtown Central City. The sidewalks are full with people enjoying the day.

Suddenly, the villain Captain Cold appears. His large blue Husky, Admiral Peary, follows behind him.

Captain Cold is carrying a giant ice blaster. He kicks open the door of a jewelry store.

Everyone inside is blasted with ice! No one can move.

Captain Cold strolls into the store.

He grabs the world-famous Ice-Blue

Diamond. Then he leaves.

The Flash zooms up the street after

the villain.

Captain Cold aims his blaster at the sidewalk. He creates a mound of ice followed by an ice sheet.

The Flash trips over the mound and slips on the ice sheet. He loses his balance and crashes into a building.

"I hope you had a nice trip," says Captain Cold. "Or should I say *slip*?" Then he and Admiral Peary run away.

The Flash speaks into a small device. "Whatzit. Are you there? I need you!" he says.

CHAPTER 2

Terrific Turtle Time

The Fastest Turtle Alive is there in seconds. Whatzit has come to help his friend!

The Flash runs to the jewelry store to thaw out the clerks.

Whatzit rushes down the street after Captain Cold and Admiral Peary.

Captain Cold aims his ice blaster

at Whatzit.

The superpowered turtle is

trapped inside a giant ice cube!

Whatzit watches Captain Cold walk away.

Then the quick-thinking hero realizes that he can still wiggle his feet.

Whatzit starts moving his feet faster and faster. His super-fast feet heat up the ice and cause it to melt.

Whatzit is freed!

Captain Cold is nowhere to be seen.

But his dog, Admiral Peary, has stayed

behind.

Whatzit sprints straight toward the growling dog.

Admiral Peary opens his mouth wide, ready to bite Whatzit.

The dog's jaws snap shut. But Whatzit is no longer there! The speedy turtle is leaping through the air.

The dog jumps and tries to catch Whatzit. But he loses his balance and tumbles backward.

Admiral Peary crashes into a fire hydrant and knocks himself out.

CHAPTER 3

What a Whirl

Down the street, the sound of an

alarm fills the air.

BRRRRIIIIIINGGGG!

Captain Cold exits a bank with a bag full of cash. He sees Whatzit rushing toward him.

"Not you again," says the villain. He aims his ice blaster.

This time, Whatzit is ready. He zooms over and runs in circles around the Super-Villain.

Captain Cold spins like a top. He is trapped inside Whatzit's whirling air currents.

The ice blaster flies from his hands.
It lands on the ground and breaks into
tiny pieces.

The dizzy villain finally stops spinning. He drops to the ground and passes out.

The Flash arrives. He takes the bag of cash and the diamond from the villain.

When Captain Cold wakes up, he finds himself tied up. He scowls at the two heroes.

"Don't look so sad, Captain Cold," says The Flash with a smile. "Thanks to one fast-moving and fast-thinking turtle, you'll have plenty of time to chill out in prison."

AUTHOR!

Steve Korté is the author of many books for children and young adults. He worked at DC Comics for many years, editing more than 600 books about Superman, Batman, Wonder Woman, and the other heroes and villains in the DC Universe. He lives in New York City with his husband, Bill, and their super-cat, Duke.

ILLUSTRATOR!

Famous cartoonist Art Baltazar is the creative force behind *The New York Times* bestselling, Eisner Award-winning DC Comics' Tiny Titans; co-writer for Billy Batson and the Magic of Shazam, Young Justice, Green Lantern Animated (Comic); and artist/co-writer for the awesome Tiny Titans/Little Archie crossover, Superman Family Adventures, Super Powers, and Itty Bitty Hellboy! Art is one of the founders of Aw Yeah Comics comic shop and the ongoing comic series. Aw yeah, living the dream! He stays home and draws comics and never has to leave the house! He lives with his lovely wife, Rose, sons Sonny and Gordon, and daughter, Audrey! AW YEAH MAN! Visit him at www.artbaltazar.com

"Word Power"

balance (BA-luhnts)—the ability to keep steady and not fall over

current (KUHR-uhnt)—the action of something moving constantly in one direction

device (di-VYSE)—a machine that does a specific job

diamond (DY-muhnd)—a hard, colorless stone that is worth a lot of money and often used in jewelry

scowl (SKOWL)—to look unhappy and angry

sprint (SPRINT)—to run very fast for a short distance

thaw (THAW)—to change from frozen to liquid

villain (VIL-uhn)—an evil or bad person who is often a character in a story

WRITING PROMPTS

1. Imagine you were in the jewelry store when Captain Cold attacked. Write a story from your point of view. How did it feel to get frozen? How did The Flash save you?

2. What if you could have a superpowered pet? What animal would it be? What powers would it have? Write a paragraph about it, then try drawing a picture.

3. Make a wanted poster for Captain Cold. Be sure to list details that will help people spot the villain!

DISCUSSION QUESTIONS

1. Whatzit is fast on his feet, but he's also a quick thinker. If you could be super-fast or super-smart, which would choose? Why?

2. Whatzit charges toward the growling Admiral Peary. Do you think the turtle was nervous? How would you have felt? Would you have faced the Husky head-on or tried to run around him?

3. The Flash and Whatzit work together to save the day. Talk about a time a friend helped you. How did it go?

THE AMAZING ADVENTURES OF THE DC SUPER-PETS!

Collect them all!